Dear Parents:

Children learn to read in stages, and all children develop reading skills at different ages. **Ready Readers**™ were created to promote children's interest in reading and to increase their reading skills. **Ready Readers**™ are written on two levels to accommodate children ranging in age from three through eight. These stages are meant to be used only as a guide.

Stage 1: Preschool-Grade 1
Stage 1 books are written in very short, simple sentences with large type. They are perfect for children who are getting ready to read or are just becoming familiar with reading on their own.

Stage 2: Grades 1-3
Stage 2 books have longer sentences and are a bit more complex. They are suitable for children who are able to read but still may need help.

All the **Ready Readers**™ tell varied, easy-to-follow stories and are colorfully illustrated. Reading will be fun, and soon your child will not only be ready, but eager to read.

No Snow for Seth

Written by Jean Davis Callaghan

Illustrated by Mikke Wotton

Modern Publishing
A Division of Unisystems, Inc.
New York, New York 10022

"Why is the snow melting?"
Seth asks his mother.

"Winter is over," says Mother, "until next year."

Seth plays outside in the snow all day.

He gets an idea.
He puts some snow in a big jar.

He puts the jar of snow
into the freezer.

Now Seth has snow to play with all year round.

He makes snowballs,
and snow houses.

He makes little snowmen.

At night, he dreams about snow, and what fun he will have when winter comes again.

"It's warm today," says Mother. "How about coming outside with me?"

"No, thank you," says Seth. "I will stay inside and play with my snow."

Seth wonders, "What could
Mother be doing out there?"
He runs outside to see.

Mother is working in the garden.
"The seeds you planted grew
into flowers!" Seth cries.

Seth helps Mother tend
the flowers.

"Oh, no! My snow!" Seth cries.
"I left the jar on the table!"
He runs back inside.

The snow has melted.
Now it is just water.

"The flowers need water,"
Mother says.

Seth pours some of the water onto the flowers.

Then he pours some
onto his toes!

It feels nice and cool.

"I have fun in the winter,"
says Seth.
"And now I'll have fun
in the spring!"